RUSS THOMPSON

FINDING HOME

Finding Forward

Books

Published by Finding Forward Books.
P.O. Box 8182, Long Beach, California 90808.
www.findingforwardbooks.com

Editing by Laura Perkins. Series concept by
Pam Sheppard. Text set in Open Dyslexic Mono.

LCCN: 2024910651
ISBN: 979-8-9890657-6-9 (paperback)
ISBN: 979-8-9890657-7-6 (ebook)
FILE: FF011-19E-20250308

Summary: A homeless tenth grader who lives in
a car with his mom strives to succeed in
school and build a better life for himself.

BISAC Subject Codes: | YOUNG ADULT FICTION /
Social Themes / Poverty and Homelessness
YOUNG ADULT FICTION / Social Themes /
Emotions and Feelings

Lexile readability measure: HL530L

For Betty Jean,

our kids,

and grandkids.

CONTENTS

1 ONLY BOOKS

MONDAY MORNING. Dover Park. The sun hits me in the face because the sheet doesn't cover the window all the way.

I look to my left.

Mom is gone.

She's probably still in Cappy's van.

I grab my clean clothes from the back seat and walk across the parking lot to the men's restroom.

It's filthy, and the floor is wet. But I'm used to it now because

we've been living here for almost
two months.

I wash myself in the sink, put on
my clean clothes, and wash my dirty
clothes from yesterday.

It's cold. But at least I'm
clean.

I go back to the car and hang my
wet clothes on the string over the
back seat.

It's time to leave for school.

I grab my backpack, lock the car,
and begin walking.

I'm fifteen now.

I wonder what I'll be doing when
I'm sixteen.

EDISON HIGH SCHOOL. I get to the
food court, show my ID card to get
breakfast, and find a table in the
sun.

It's Monday, so they have coffee
cake. I eat it slowly to get all the
flavor.

I remember the coffee cake that
Mom used to make. There was nothing
better.

I look up and see Olive. She
studies at the table across from me.

I have her in math and English.

She's pretty, and she lives on
the good side of Conroy.

I've never had the courage to
talk to her.

MATH. I get there early, sit down,
and wait for class to start.

Mr. Braden hands back our tests.

Most of the students smile when
they see their grades.

But not me.

Mine is a D.

No matter how hard I try, I just can't get it.

AFTER SCHOOL. Library. I sit at a table in the back.

I don't get much work done. But I like coming here because it's clean and quiet.

The clock says five.

"See you all tomorrow," Ms. Ensley says. "Time to go home."

I begin the walk back to Dover Park.

It's not home.

It's where I stay.

DOVER PARK. Mom is sleeping with her mouth open when I get to the car.

She used to look young. But her teeth are turning brown. And the skin on her face looks like dried

4

Leather.

I open the door, sit next to her,
and try not to think about it.

The meth is killing her.

TEN MINUTES PASS. Mom sits up
straight. "We need to go."

"Where to?" I ask.

"We need to make some money."

We leave the parking lot.

I know what's coming next.

I don't like it.

FIVE MINUTES LATER. We cross under
the train bridge to the good side of
Conroy.

The people here get a lot of
expensive deliveries.

Mom slows down. "Doyle, look at
the yellow house. There's a box on
the porch."

She pulls to the curb. I start to get out.

But a man opens the front door and picks up the box.

We drive around to some other streets. But there's nothing more to take.

In a way, I'm glad.

I think back to what happened on Saturday.

It was raining. We pulled up to a house on Gilbert Street that had a box in front.

I walked up to the porch and grabbed it like I always do.

But a guy came out and chased me.

I ran as fast as I could.

I thought he was going to catch me.

But he slipped on the wet sidewalk and fell.

I jumped in the car, and Mom
floored it.

We were lucky to get away.

When I opened the box, there was
nothing we could sell.

It was only books.

2 CAN'T STAND

LATER. We cross under the train bridge and head back to Dover Park.

"Too bad we didn't get anything," Mom says. "Maybe we can get something tomorrow."

What she really means is that she wanted something she could give to Cappy.

I think about his van in the parking lot.

I can't stand him.

There's a green light ahead. But Mom slows down.

"What's happening?" I ask.

"Doyle, be cool," she says. "There's a police car behind us."

I turn around and see the red lights flashing.

Mom pulls to the curb and stops the motor.

"Keep your hands where the cops can see them," she says. "Do whatever they say. Don't make any quick moves."

The first cop comes to Mom's window. The second one stands behind us.

"Do you know why we pulled you over?" the first cop asks.

"Is it because of all the stuff in the back?" asks Mom.

"It's blocking your rear window," he says. "It's a safety hazard."

I watch as he checks out our

stuff in the back. I think about how
it's everything we own.

"Are you moving?" the cop asks.

"We got put out of our
apartment," Mom says. "We're going
to my sister's house."

"Where is that?"

"About a mile from here."

He looks at both of us. I feel
myself sweating.

"I'm going to let you go with a
warning," he says. "Just be
careful."

The cops get back in their car
and drive away.

I wish Mom did have a sister.

Maybe then we would have a place
to live.

DINNER. Mom pulls into the parking
lot of Burger House.

The food is good here. And the bathrooms are clean.

We order off the dollar menu and take a seat by the window.

I look at the other people. They all seem happy.

"I know it's been hard," Mom says. "But we're going to get out of this once I start working again."

I know she means well. But I don't think it's going to happen.

At least we will get to have something good for dinner tonight.

And it will be nice to clean up in the bathroom.

DOVER PARK. Mom pulls into the parking lot and stops the car.

"I'll be right back," she says.

But I know she won't.

I watch as she walks to Cappy's

van.

At least I got to eat dinner tonight.

I open one of the books I got from that house on Saturday.

The title is, *I Survived Hurricane Katrina*. It's by Lauren Tarshis.

I'm on Chapter Three. I can read most of the words. It's also exciting.

LATER. The car shakes. I open my eyes.

It's the middle of the night. Mom gets into the front seat.

"We're going," she says. "We can stay in the parking lot at Price Mart."

"What happened?"

"Don't worry about it," she says.

"We have to go."

I look at my phone. It's two in the morning.

She starts the car.

I can't stand living this way.

3 REGULAR PERSON

TUESDAY MORNING. Math is my worst subject. But Olive smiles at me when I walk through the door. Maybe things will be better today.

Mr. Braden comes to the front of the classroom. "I want to say a few words about the Khan Academy," he says. "It's a website that can help you learn math. Beginning today, I'm going to make my lessons tie into it. For homework, when you get stuck, you'll be able to get help on the Khan Academy."

He clicks on his computer. The
website for the Khan Academy comes
up on the screen.

A guy with a calm voice explains
how to do a word problem. He makes
it seem simple. I can understand it.

I don't have a laptop. But I can
use a computer in the library.

Maybe the Khan Academy will help
me.

STUDY HALL. It's a double classroom
with about thirty long tables and
sixty kids. They put me in here
because I failed math and history
last semester.

Mr. Rubio comes to the front. He
looks at each of us before he begins
speaking. "I want you to know that
you are all capable of being
successful here at Edison High

School," he says. "You go step-by-step, grade-by-grade. When you finish grade twelve, you'll be ready for grade thirteen. It can be college, career training, or the military. It's there for all of you."

He makes me feel like I can do it. But when I look sideways, a guy at the next table is mad-dogging me.

He's one of the peer tutors, probably a senior.

I've seen him in the hall. He walks with a limp.

ENGLISH. Ms. Gulliver smiles when I come through the door.

She's old, and sometimes she gets cranky. But she cares about us.

The bell rings. She comes to the front.

"Take out your books to begin
sustained silent reading," she says.
"I'll be calling on you at random
when time is up."

I take out the book I got on
Saturday and begin reading.

The cover makes it look like a
kid book. I put it inside a regular
book so nobody will know.

Eighteen minutes pass.

"Time is up," Ms. Gulliver says.
She pulls a card out of her name
jar. "Doyle, what did you read?"

Normally, I would be nervous. But
not today.

"I'm reading *I Survived Hurricane
Katrina*, by Lauren Tarshis," I say.
"The main character is a young kid.
He's with his family in their car.
They're trying to get out of town
before the hurricane comes."

"Very good," Ms. Gulliver says.

I look to the side.

Olive smiles.

Maybe I should talk to her.

LUNCH. All of the tables are full when I reach the food court.

I turn to go outside. But Olive smiles and waves to me.

She sits at a table by herself. I sit across from her.

"What do you think about math?" she asks.

"I don't know. But the Khan Academy seems like it might be good."

"What about Ms. Gulliver?" she asks.

"She's nice. I wish all of my teachers could be like her."

"I know what you mean," Olive

says. "My big brother liked Ms. Gulliver, too."

The more we talk, the better I feel.

She may be pretty and live on the good side of town.

But she seems like a regular person.

4 ONE OF THEM

THURSDAY. Math. It's one week later.
Mr. Braden shakes my hand when I get
to the door.

"Doyle," he says. "Good job on
the test yesterday."

"Thanks," I say. "The Khan
Academy is really helping me. I can
understand the way that Khan guy
explains things."

I've seen Mr. Braden shake hands
with other kids. But I never thought
he would shake hands with me.

STUDY HALL. The bell rings to begin class. Mr. Rubio comes to the front.

"I'm changing your work partners today," he says. "If you're a tutor, I will call out the number of your new table."

He calls out names. The tutors start switching places. The guy who comes to my table is the one who has been mad-dogging me.

I reach out to give him a fist bump. He acts like he doesn't see it.

"I'm Perry," he says.

"I'm Doyle."

"What are you working on?" he asks.

"Math."

"Go ahead and start," he says. "I'll watch while you do it."

I begin working. I try my

hardest. But I don't know what to
do.

"Read the problem to yourself one
more time," he says. "Then I'll take
you through the steps."

I read the problem again and try
to understand it. But I can't.

Then it happens. Something about
Perry changes. He reads the problem
to me in a patient way and shows me
how to do it.

I begin working and finish it. I
understand it now.

"Good job," Perry says.

I wonder what made him change.

LUNCH. Olive waits for me at the
food lines.

We get our lunches and walk to
the outside benches. We've been
sitting together for a week.

That's when I see Perry.

I give him a thumbs up. But he looks at me like he's mad again.

Olive and I find a place to sit. Forget Perry.

AFTER SCHOOL. Library. It's almost five o'clock. I sit at a computer and try to finish my math.

"Doyle, I know you want to keep working," Ms. Ensley says. "But it's time to leave."

I shut down my computer and walk out the door with the other kids.

They all have homes to go to.

I wish I could be one of them.

5 STRAIGHT AT ME

TUESDAY. Study hall. Perry walks
through the door.

His limp is worse. He gets to our
table and sits next to me.

I see the pain in his face. Maybe
that's why he looked mad during
lunch yesterday.

"Perry, thanks again for your
help," I say. "I got a C on my math
test. If I keep bringing my grades
up, maybe I can get on the track
team."

Perry smiles. "That would be

great," he says.

It has always been my dream to be in a sport.

But I never could because my grades were too low.

THE BELL RINGS. Study hall is over. Everyone leaves.

I see Perry's cell phone under his chair.

I know I can get money for it. And nobody will know if I keep it. But Perry has been helping me.

I pick up the phone and run into the hall. I catch up to him and tap him on the shoulder.

"Perry, is this yours?" I ask. "It was under your chair."

He looks at me like he can't believe what I'm doing. He reaches out to shake my hand.

"Thanks," he says. "You really saved me."

From the look in his eyes, I know he means it.

FIVE O'CLOCK. I leave the library and begin walking home.

It's been a good day at school. I feel better about things.

Soon, I'm at Dover Park. I reach our car and get in the front seat.

"Doyle, let's go," Mom says. "We have to make some money."

I don't want to do it.

But I don't have a choice.

FIVE MINUTES LATER. We get to the good side of town and turn right onto Cortland Street.

A delivery van passes by.

"Doyle, over there," Mom says.

"There's a package on the doorstep
of that yellow house."

Mom pulls to the curb.

I go to the porch, grab the box,
and walk quickly back to the car.

Nobody chases me.

Mom drives away.

We made it.

I open the box. "Mom, it's a
laptop!"

"That's great!" she says. "It's
our lucky day."

It feels good to see her smile.

But her face changes. "Close the
box," she says. "We're getting
pulled over."

I turn to look behind us. I see
two police cars with their red
lights flashing.

Mom pulls to the curb.

This feels bad. Why are there two

police cars instead of just one?

A cop comes to Mom's window.

I get a feeling that he has his hand on his gun.

"Ma'am, can I see your driver's license?" he asks.

Mom tries to act calm. But I can tell she's shaking inside.

He tells her to get out of the car. The next thing I know, he's putting handcuffs on her.

Another cop comes to my side. "Sir, I need you to get out of the car," he says.

I open the door, step out, and try not to shake.

The handcuffs click on my wrists.

I get a sick feeling in my stomach.

I watch as they search our car.

They find the stolen laptop. They

also find Mom's meth.

"We have a video of you taking the laptop," one of the cops says to me. "We put it there with a tracking device to see if someone would take it."

My heart pounds. I know we're going to jail.

That's when I see him.

It's Perry limping down the street.

He looks straight at me.

6 NO IDEA

SIDEWALK. Mom is crying with her
head down. She looks up at me.

"Doyle, I love you."

They put her into the first
police car.

"Mom, I love you, too."

They put me into the second car.

We drive away.

I look out the window.

I feel the tears come.

I can't wipe my eyes because of
the handcuffs.

POLICE STATION. They search me again
and take my picture.

I go to a lady who sits behind a
window and types into a computer.

"How do you spell your name?"

I tell her.

"What is your birthdate?"

I tell her.

"What is your address?"

"We don't have one."

The cops who arrested me take me
to a little room with scuffed-up
walls and a scratched table.

"Your mom has been arrested for
receiving stolen property,
possession of a controlled
substance, and child endangerment,"
the first cop says.

"We arrested you for grand theft
of the laptop," the second cop says.
"Is there anything you want to say?"

The tears come again. I put my
head down.

"Do you have anybody you can
call, any relatives?" the first cop
asks.

"I don't have anybody. The only
person I have is my mom."

I sit up and look into their
eyes. I can tell they feel bad.

They take me to a holding cell
with benches bolted to the floor and
two other sad-looking kids.

The second cop brings me a juice
box and a cheese sandwich.

I put it on the bench next to me.

I can't eat.

TIME PASSES. A man takes me back to
the little room with the table and
chairs.

A lady comes in with gray hair

and an old blue sweater.

"My name is Ruth Kirby," she says. "I'm going to be your social worker. Do you have anybody I can call, any relatives?"

"Just my mom."

"What about your dad?" she asks.

"He got killed in the war. It's always been just my mom and me."

Another lady comes in. She's younger and more dressed up.

"My name is Helen Hayden," she says. "I'm your attorney. I've been assigned to represent you."

The room is hot and stuffy. I wish I could get some fresh air.

"What happened?" Ms. Hayden asks me.

I tell her about losing our apartment, living in our car, and the stealing.

"What was going on with your
mom?" Ms. Kirby asks me.

"What do you mean?"

"There was meth in the car," she
says.

I don't want to tell her.

But for some reason, I do.

I tell her everything.

LATER. Two men come in and sit
across from me. I can tell they're
detectives from the badges on their
belts.

"Can you tell us what happened?"
the first one asks.

I look at Ms. Hayden. She nods
for me to start.

I tell the story again. I can see
they feel bad about what has
happened to me.

"I'm sorry about what you're

going through," the first detective says. "If you really want to know, we're on your side."

It surprises me to hear him say that. But I'm still glad when they leave.

Ms. Kirby looks at me. "The next thing that will happen, is that you will be going to live with a foster family."

"There will also be a court case," Ms. Hayden says. "You will appear before a judge in about a month. You will probably just get probation."

They're trying to be nice. But I feel myself shaking again.

They have no idea what I'm going through.

7 WITH MOM

HOLDING CELL. I look through the bars at the guard sitting behind the desk.

He has a look on his face like he's dead inside.

That's how I feel, too.

But it's not just because I'm in jail.

It's because there's nothing for me.

I'm all alone.

I see Mom in my head. I remember the look on her face when they arrested her.

I remember the look on her face when we lost our apartment.

I remember the look on her face when she would come back high from Cappy's van.

I think about Dad. He was a sergeant in the Army.

But he's dead now. I never even knew him.

It used to be nice with Mom. She had a job. We had a good place to live.

Then she started using meth.

Everything is gone now.

TIME PASSES. The guard says I'm going to be released.

I follow him down the hallway. Ms. Kirby is there.

"Doyle, first, we're going to get

something to eat," she says. "Then
I'm taking you to the Jensen's.
That's where you're going to stay
tonight."

We go outside. It feels good to
breathe the fresh air.

But what are the Jensens like?
Where will I be tomorrow?

EVENING. Golden Grill. I open the
door for Ms. Kirby. We go inside and
sit in the back.

"Do you know where my mom is?" I
ask.

"I checked," Ms. Kirby says.
"They took her to county jail."

"Do you know when I'll be able to
see her?"

"I don't know," she says. "But
I'll call."

"Do you know when they'll let her

out?"

"If she makes bail, they'll release her right away. But if she doesn't, she'll be there until her trial."

"How long will that be?"

Ms. Kirby sighs. "It could be months."

I turn away so she can't see the look on my face.

Mom has no money.

She will never make bail.

TEN O'CLOCK. Ms. Kirby drives down Willard Street.

I know it well. The houses are old. Dover Park is only two blocks away.

She stops in front of a tan house with flowers in front.

"The Jensens are good people,"

Ms. Kirby says. "They have two other
foster kids. I think you're going to
like it here."

I get out of the car, grab my
backpack, and follow Ms. Kirby.

The front door opens when we get
to the porch. Mr. and Mrs. Jensen
come out with smiles on their faces.

Mr. Jensen is tall, like he used
to be a basketball player.

He reaches out to shake my hand.
When I look in his eyes, I can tell
he's glad to see me.

It's the same with Mrs. Jensen.
She doesn't know me. But I can tell
she cares.

We go inside. The furniture is
old and the carpet is worn. But
everything is clean.

It feels like home.

When they show me my bedroom, I

get the same feeling.

It's real.

And it's for me.

LATER. I take a shower and put on
the pajamas Mrs. Jensen gave me.

Then I wash my clothes and hang
them in the shower so I can be ready
for tomorrow.

The Jensens are nice.

But I feel alone.

I wish I could be with Mom.

8 WANT ME

TUESDAY MORNING. I open my eyes. I don't know where I am.

Then I remember.

There's a knock on the door. "Doyle, it's time to get up," Ms. Jensen says. "We have breakfast for you."

I get up to get my clothes from the bathroom.

But they're dried and folded outside my door when I open it.

I guess Mrs. Jensen washed them.

BREAKFAST. Mrs. Jensen is sitting with the other foster kids when I get to the kitchen table.

The guy looks like he's in middle school, but he's tall. He gets up and pulls out a chair for me. "I'm Mario," he says. "This seat is for you."

I sit down and put my napkin in my lap.

The girl looks like she's in grade school. But she's also tall. "I'm Inez," she says. "You're going to like it here."

I put corn flakes in my bowl and pour some milk in.

"Doyle, did you sleep okay last night?" Mrs. Jensen asks.

"It was great," I say. "Thanks for washing my clothes."

The front door opens. Mr. Jensen

walks in and sits at the kitchen
table.

He's wearing blue work jeans and
a sweaty T-shirt that says Price
Mart. He's tired, like he's been
working all night.

"How was the warehouse?" Mrs.
Jensen asks him.

"It was fine," Mr. Jensen says.
"They put us through some new safety
training."

Mrs. Jensen gets up and takes her
dishes to the sink. She looks fresh,
wearing shined work shoes and a
creased shirt that says Food Giant
Market.

I finish eating and look at the
clock. It's after seven.

"I'm taking you all to school
this morning," Mr. Jensen says.
"We'll be getting out of here in

twenty minutes."

They all seem normal and happy, like how it was before things went bad with Mom.

SEVEN-THIRTY. Inez, Mario, and I go out to the car with Mr. Jensen.

He drives a white Nissan, just like Mom's. The only difference is that it's shiny, and it doesn't have a big dent on the side.

I open the back door to get in.

"Doyle, that's okay," Mr. Jensen says. "This is your day for the front seat."

I go around to the front. We all get in. Mr. Jensen pulls out of the driveway.

Our first stop is Longfellow Elementary School.

Inez opens her door. "Doyle, have

a good day," she says.

She climbs out of the car and runs to the front gate.

Our next stop is Keller Middle School.

Mario gives me a fist bump. "Doyle, see you after school," he says.

Edison High School is next. Mr. Jensen parks when we get there.

"We have to go to the office," he says. "I need to fill out some forms to say you'll be living with us."

I feel relieved to hear him say that.

I wasn't sure they would want me.

9 WISH I WAS

WEDNESDAY. Study hall. I don't want
to see Perry.

I don't want him to know why I
was arrested. I don't want him to
know I was homeless. And I don't
want him to know about Mom.

He comes through the door and
limps to our table.

"Doyle, what happened?" he asks.

I lean forward and put my head
down. "I don't want to talk about
it."

Minutes pass. Mr. Rubio comes to

our table. "Doyle, what's wrong?"

I keep my head down and say nothing.

"Are you ill?" he asks.

I raise my head and try to look sick. "I feel like I might throw up."

He writes me a pass and sends me to the nurse.

It feels good to get out of there.

ENGLISH. Ms. Gulliver stands at the door and smiles when I get to her classroom.

The bell rings. She comes to the front.

"Take out your books for sustained silent reading," she says. "Get started now."

I open my book, *I Survived the*

California Wildfires, by Lauren Tarshis.

It's another one of the books I got from that porch.

The kid in the story is in a forest and surrounded by fire. He doesn't know where to go.

In a way, I know how he feels.

LUNCH. Olive is waiting for me when I get to the food court.

I try to act like everything is okay.

She reaches out to hold my hand while we stand in line to get our lunches. We get our food and go to the outside benches.

"Doyle, is something wrong?" she asks.

"It's bad," I say. "This has to stay between you and me."

I tell her about the arrest.

I tell her that Mom is in jail.

And I tell her that I'm staying with the Jensens.

I see tears in her eyes.

I reach out to hold her hand.

PHYSICAL EDUCATION. I walk to the track with the rest of the class and step up to the starting line.

"One mile," Mr. Quinty says. "Ready, go."

I usually start out fast and come in first.

But today, I hang back with the slow people and take my time.

I think about Mom and what she's going through. I also think about the future. I don't know what's going to happen to me.

I'm almost last when I cross the

finish line.

"Doyle, you're the fastest guy in all of my classes," Mr. Quinty says. "Are you okay?"

I don't know what to say.

I wish I was.

10 SHORT GUY

AFTERNOON. Five o'clock. I leave the library to walk home.

The quiet is nice. It gives me time to think.

Then Mom comes into my head.

I wish she wasn't locked up. But at least she can't get meth now.

I think about how she was destroying herself. I saw what it was doing to her every day.

It was also destroying me.

I reach Willard Street and walk up the front steps to the Jensens' house.

It's a good place. And the Jensens are nice people.

I hope I can stay here until Mom gets out.

LATER. I lie on my bed. There's a knock on the door.

Mario comes in. "Doyle, do you want to shoot hoops?"

The Jensens have a basketball hoop bolted to their garage. We go out to the driveway and begin shooting.

Mario is younger than me, but about two inches taller. I feel short next to him.

He sinks a jumper from fifteen feet like it's the easiest thing in the world.

I get the rebound and try to do

the same. But I miss.

The ball goes back to Mario. He sinks another one.

"Inez and I have been here for two years," he says.

"What happened?" I ask.

He misses the next shot. "It's a long story," he says. "But we like it here."

He goes in for a reverse layup and makes it look easy.

"What about you?" Mario asks.

"It's a long story for me, too."

I grab the ball and put up another shot. It bounces off the rim.

"What's it like here?" I ask.

"There are three rules," Mario says. "You have to do your homework. You have to be in a sport. And you have to help around the house."

54

"What's the big deal about sports?"

"Mr. and Mrs. Jensen both played basketball in high school," he says. "They say it did a lot for them."

I miss another jump shot. "I've always wanted to run track. But my grades have never been good enough."

"That used to be me," Mario says. "But my grades are okay now. What do you do in track?"

"I don't know. But when we run in PE, I always come in first."

Mario puts up another shot. It goes right in.

"When you talk to Mr. and Mrs. Jensen, what do you call them?" I ask.

"They told us we could use their first names. But we call them Mr. and Mrs. Jensen."

We continue shooting hoops.

I'm pretty terrible.

But Mario gives me some tips.

"Doyle, you're not too bad for a short guy," he says.

11 ALONE

SIX O'CLOCK. Dinner. Mr. Jensen comes through the front door with two giant pizzas.

We go to the kitchen and sit down to eat.

"Kids, how was your day?" Mr. Jensen asks.

"I miss basketball," Mario says. "But volleyball is going good so far."

"I hit a double in softball today," Inez says. "We have our first game in two weeks."

"Doyle, what about you?" Mrs.
Jensen asks.

"It was a regular day, just
classes."

"That's good," she says. "We had
a nice day at Food Giant."

"Last night was good for me too,"
Mr. Jensen says. "Everything at the
warehouse went fine."

Mrs. Jensen opens the pizza
boxes.

Everyone is talking, smiling, and
laughing.

It's the best pizza I've had in a
long time.

TEN O'CLOCK. I sit at the kitchen
table doing math. Mr. Jensen is at
work now. Mrs. Jensen comes into the
kitchen.

"When are you going to bed?" she

asks.

"Pretty soon. I just have a little more."

"The doors are locked," she says. "But check one more time before you go to bed. See you in the morning."

She leaves the kitchen. The house gets quiet.

It feels calm and safe here.

TEN-THIRTY. I finish studying for the math test tomorrow.

I should be tired. But I still can't sleep.

There's a mockingbird singing outside. I open the kitchen door and go out so I can hear it better.

I close the door behind me, sit on the back steps, and look into the tree.

I can't see the mockingbird. But

I know it's there.

I wish Mom could hear it.

I get up to go back inside.

The door is locked.

I go around to the front door.

It's locked, too.

I tap on Mario's window.

Nothing.

I tap again.

He must be fast asleep.

There's no way I'm going to wake
Mrs. Jensen.

I return to the back steps.

The mockingbird keeps singing.

I feel alone.

12 WHAT IF?

THURSDAY MORNING. It's five-thirty
when Mario finally hears me tapping
on his window.

I'm shivering when he opens the
back door.

"Doyle, what happened?" he asks.

"It's a long story. I locked
myself out."

It's a relief to get inside. I
was worried that Mrs. Jensen was
going to catch me.

I take a hot shower, get dressed,
and go out to breakfast.

Mr. Jensen comes in the front door. He looks tired from working all night.

"Doyle, how come you're yawning so much?" he asks.

"I don't know. But I slept good."

"Are you okay for walking to school with Mario and Inez today?" he asks.

"Yeah, I'm fine."

"By the way, here's your door key," he says. "I meant to give it to you last night. It works on the front door, the gate, and the back door."

Mario smiles. "Doyle, that's good. Now you don't have to worry about getting locked out."

SEVEN O'CLOCK. Mario, Inez, and I leave the house and walk down the sidewalk to school.

I try not to yawn. But I can't
help it.

The first school we reach is
Longfellow. Mario and I wait on the
sidewalk until Inez gets inside.

"Doyle, what happened last
night?" Mario asks.

"I stepped outside to get some
air. But I accidentally locked the
door behind me."

"Why didn't you knock on my
window?" he asks.

"I was tapping all night. But you
didn't wake up."

"How come you didn't knock hard?"
he asks.

"No way. I didn't want to wake up
Mrs. Jensen."

"You need to lighten up," Mario
says. "She probably would have

laughed."

I guess he's right. But I wasn't thinking that at the time.

I catch myself yawning again.

I wish I didn't have a test in math today.

MATH. Mr. Braden comes to the front of the classroom.

"Clear your desks for the test," he says. "If you finish early, check your answers."

I never used to check my answers in the past because I never knew what I was doing.

But it's different now. I have a chance to get a good grade.

He passes out the test papers.

The first question looks easy.

I feel my eyes close.

Somebody taps my shoulder.

I look up. It's Mr. Braden. I sit up straight and open my eyes wide.

The next question is another easy one. So is the next one.

I close my eyes to rest again.

Someone taps my shoulder.

"Doyle, what's going on?" Mr. Braden asks. "You were sleeping pretty hard."

"I don't know."

"I'm going to send you to the nurse," he says. "You can take the test tomorrow."

"That's okay," I say. "It won't happen again."

"The nurse will call your parent," he says. "You might be getting sick."

I don't want to leave. But I don't have a choice.

HALLWAY. The health office is straight ahead.

But there's no way I can go there. The first thing the nurse will do is call Mr. Jensen.

I walk outside to the food court.

That's when I see Mr. Dirzo, the campus supervisor.

He waves for me to come over and show him my pass.

"How come you're out here if your pass is to the nurse?" he asks.

"I was on my way. I just needed some fresh air."

"Sure you did."

HEALTH OFFICE. The nurse gets on the phone as soon as Mr. Dirzo brings me in.

"Hi, Mr. Jensen?" she asks. "Doyle is here from his math class.

The teacher wrote a note saying that
he fell asleep twice during first
period."

She passes the phone to Mr.
Dirzo.

"I found him out on the campus,"
Mr. Dirzo says. "He'll be getting
three days of detention."

They act like they're trying to
help me.

But they don't know what they're
doing.

What if Mr. Jensen calls my
social worker?

What if I have to leave and go to
another foster home?

13 I KNOW

LATER. I leave the health office. I asked Mr. Jensen to let me stay at school, and he said I could.

I walk to study hall and take my seat.

I know this class is helping me. And I want to stay at Edison.

But there's no point.

I shouldn't have ditched. The Jensens are going to get rid of me.

All they have to do is call Ms. Kirby.

I look up and see Perry as he

comes through the door of the study
hall.

He's walking on crutches today.
He comes to our table and sits down.

"What happened?" I ask.

"I tried to run yesterday," Perry
says. "But I hurt my knee again."

"What do you mean?"

"I run the 3200 meters on the
track team," he says. "But I messed
up my knee. I was hoping to make it
to the state track finals this year.
But it's not going to happen."

He looks at me funny, like he's
waiting for me to say something.

"Doyle, did things get any better
after that thing with the police?"
he asks.

It's none of his business.
There's nothing I have to say.

"You don't know this," Perry

says. "But Olive is my sister. She told me what happened."

I should have known that I couldn't trust her. How could I have been so stupid?

"I'm sorry about what you're going through," Perry says. "I truly am."

I say nothing. I don't want to talk about it.

"Do you remember three weeks ago on Saturday?" Perry asks.

"What do you mean?"

"We live on Gilbert Street," he says. "It was raining. I was looking out the window when you snatched a package off our porch. I slipped on the sidewalk when I chased after you. That's how I hurt my knee."

I remember what happened. But I didn't know it was Perry chasing me.

He reaches out to shake my hand. "But it's not your fault," he says. "I don't blame you for it."

I don't see how he can feel that way. It was my fault.

I want to leave and never come back.

LUNCH. I don't see Olive when I get to the food court.

Good.

I go to the food line, get my lunch, and walk the opposite way from where we normally sit.

I thought I could trust her to keep her mouth shut about me.

But I was wrong.

THE BELL RINGS. School lets out.

There's no point in going to the library. I walk to the front gate.

The other kids are smiling and
Laughing.
They're happy to go home.
But not me.
Everything is clear now.
I know what I have to do.

14 I WISH

LATER. Perry's house. I walk to the porch with the books I stole.

I reach the front door, hang the bag on the doorknob, and hurry back to the sidewalk.

They were good books. But I don't want anything stolen from Perry.

I walk quickly, turn left at the corner, and cut down the alley.

DOVER PARK. My phone buzzes. It's a text from Mr. Jensen. He wants to know where I am.

I know I should answer. But I
need to think.

I sit against a tree and watch a
little-league baseball practice.

One coach hits ground balls to
the infielders.

The other coach hits fly balls to
the outfielders.

I wish I could go back in time
and be one of those kids.

I've never been on a team.

That's why track was going to be
a good sport for me.

You don't have to know anything.
You just run.

But now that I'm messing up in
school again, it doesn't matter.

There won't be any sports for me.

ALMOST DARK. I look at the parking
lot. A white Nissan drives slowly up

and down the rows.

It's Mr. Jensen.

I hide behind some bushes and keep watching.

I never thought he would come looking for me.

I figured he would just call Ms. Kirby and let it go.

I think about how it used to be.

I wish our car was there.

I wish I was sitting in the front seat with Mom.

15 FIND ME

SIX O'CLOCK. My phone buzzes again.
It's the seventh text from Mr.
Jensen. He says he's worried about
me.

I don't know what to say. I still
need time to think about things.

BURGER HOUSE. I stand at the door
and look inside.

I'm hungry. But all I have is
ninety cents.

That's when I see the headlights.
It's a white Nissan.

Mr. Jensen pulls up next to me.
"Hey Doyle, do you want to get
something to eat?"

I thought he would be mad at me.
But he doesn't sound mad at all. And
when he gets out of the car, he hugs
me.

We go inside, place our orders,
and sit at a table by the window.

"I'm glad you're okay," he says.
"We were worried."

I take a sip of soda. "I'm sorry
about not coming home. Things
started getting to me."

He looks out the window. Then he
turns to look back at me.

"You don't know much about me,"
he says. "But my parents died when I
was twelve. My aunt and uncle raised
me. But they didn't want me."

He takes a sip of coffee. "I also

had problems in school. It was hard
for me to learn. The teachers
thought I was lazy. But a teacher in
high school helped me. It's because
of her that I graduated."

It's hard for me to believe that
he ever had problems. In a way, it
makes me feel good.

"I know that things have been
hard for you," Mr. Jensen says. "But
the thing you have to remember is
that you can get through it. And you
don't have to do it alone."

It's a lot to think about.

But he did search for me.

And he did find me.

16 SCARES ME

SATURDAY MORNING. Breakfast is over. I sit at the kitchen table and look out the front window.

Ms. Kirby parks and comes to the door. It's going to be bad.

Mr. and Mrs. Jensen bring her into the kitchen.

I try not to be nervous when they leave to the living room.

"Doyle, can you tell me what happened?" Ms. Kirby asks.

I know I shouldn't lie. But I don't want to tell her everything.

"My tutor in study hall is always
getting on my case. He said I was
being lazy. I just couldn't take it
anymore. When school got out, I
needed to think about things."

"Where did you go?" she asks.

"Dover Park. I sat under a tree
by the baseball field."

Her eyes peer into me. I feel
like she's trying to read my mind.

"I know you've been through some
tough times," she says. "And the
Jensens like you. But if something
like this happens again, you will
not be able to stay here."

I can breathe now.

I thought she was going to move
me today.

AFTER LUNCH. Mario and I shoot hoops
in the driveway.

Mrs. Jensen opens the back door. She's holding her cell phone. "Doyle, it's a call for you."

It seems strange that someone would be calling me on Mrs. Jensen's cell phone. But she sounds excited.

I toss the basketball to Mario and put the phone to my ear.

"Doyle! Hi honey!"

"Mom!"

There's a pause on the phone. I hear loud voices in the background.

Mom starts talking again. "Ms. Kirby told me you didn't come home after school on Thursday. What's going on?"

"I'm sorry. I know I shouldn't have done that. It will never happen again."

I hear more voices in the background. It sounds like echoing.

"Mom, what about you?" I ask.
"Are you okay?"

"I'm feeling better," she says.
"In a way, I'm glad I'm here."

I think about what the meth was
doing to her. I hope it's true that
she's getting better.

"Do you know when you'll be
getting out?" I ask.

"It's going to be a while," she
says. "There's no money for bail.
And I still don't have a trial
date."

"Do you know when I can come and
see you?"

"Maybe in about a week," she
says. "Mr. Jensen told me he would
bring you."

A week seems so long. I wish I
could see her now.

"You have to promise me

something," Mom says. "You have to do whatever Mr. and Mrs. Jensen tell you to do. And no more running away. You're lucky to be with them. You might have to be there for a long time."

It hits me hard when she says that.

She's my mom.

I don't know how long I can take being away from her.

DRIVEWAY. Mario sinks a jumper from the left.

"I know why you stayed away," he says. "Sometimes, things get to me, too."

"What happened?" I ask.

"My mom got sent to prison for credit-card fraud. She won't be out for three more years."

"Do you ever get to see her?" I
ask.

"Inez and I have seen her twice.
The prison where she's at is three-
hundred miles away."

"How do you deal with it?" I ask.

"I know her release date," he
says. "I check off the days on a
calendar. I just try my best to keep
going."

I put up a shot from the right.
It bounces off the rim.

Mario grabs the ball and sinks it
like he always does.

I'm glad I can talk to him.

TEN O'CLOCK. I lie on my bed reading
a book I got from Ms. Gulliver.

My door is open. I hear Mrs.
Jensen watching the news.

It's a story about a homeless guy

84

on meth.

He gets arrested and they lock
him up. But as soon as he gets out,
he starts using again.

It scares me.

17 OPENED FOR ME

MONDAY MORNING. Food court. I get my breakfast and look for a place to sit.

I see Olive.

I would like to sit with her.

But I think about the books I stole and what I did to her brother. I just can't face her.

I turn the other way and leave.

STUDY HALL. Perry looks happy when he walks in.

But I have no idea what he could

be happy about.

His knee is messed up. He can't run track. And it's all because of me.

He sits down and opens his backpack. I can tell he's excited.

"Doyle, my mom sent these for you," he says.

He takes out a bunch of paperbacks. They're like the ones I stole from his porch, but the titles are different.

"What are these for?" I ask.

"My mom teaches middle school. These are some spare books she had. Also, she says thanks for the books you brought back."

The books he's giving me are brand new. I don't want to take them. I don't like being a charity case.

But I'll return them as soon as I
read them.

It's strange.

All of a sudden, people are doing
nice things for me.

PHYSICAL EDUCATION. Mr. Quinty
finishes taking attendance and faces
us.

"Before we get started, I need to
say a few things," he says. "It's
something I've been thinking about
for a while."

I wonder what he's going to say.
He doesn't usually give speeches.

"I was talking with my nephew on
Saturday," Mr. Quinty says. "He told
me that he lost his warehouse job
because he was making too many
mistakes. I felt bad for him and
told him to keep trying. But he said

he was tired of getting knocked down
all the time."

Mr. Quinty walks back and forth
in front of us. I feel it when he
looks at me.

"We all get discouraged," he
says. "And we all get knocked down.
But you can't succeed if you give
up. You can only succeed if you get
up and keep trying."

I know he means well.

But I'm not his nephew.

Sometimes it doesn't matter how
hard you try.

AFTER SCHOOL. Locker room. It's
crowded and noisy with all the
sports guys getting ready for
practice.

Some of them are joking around
and laughing. I wish I could be one

of them.

Perry said I should talk to Mr. Quinty about practicing with the track team.

I feel myself shaking when I knock on the door of the PE office.

Mr. Quinty looks up from his desk. "Doyle, come in," he says.

I don't know what to say. But I only have a chance if I try.

"I know my report card wasn't good enough for me to be on the track team this year," I say. "But my grades are starting to come up now. I was wondering if I could practice with the track team."

"What kind of grades do you have?" Mr. Quinty asks.

"I have a C or higher in everything except math."

"How are you going to bring up

your math grade?"

"I have study hall during second period. A guy in there is helping me. I've also been working after school in the library on this website called the Khan Academy."

Mr. Quinty looks me in the eye. "I've never done anything like this before. But the grading deadline for the next report card is in two weeks. You can run during track practice if you get a C or higher in everything by the deadline."

I feel myself smiling when I leave the PE office.

A door has been opened for me.

18 PRACTICE

MONDAY MORNING. Edison High School. I walk through the front gate.

Two weeks have passed since I talked to Mr. Quinty.

Today is the deadline to turn in work for the next report card.

If I get a C or higher in every class, I can practice with the track team.

The class I'm worried about is math. We had a test on Friday, and it was hard.

MATH. The bell rings. Mr. Braden comes to the front of the classroom.

"I finished grading your tests last night," he says. "Most of you did well. But some of you had a hard time. If you think you might be in trouble for your report card grade, there's an extra assignment on the board. You have to get it done by five o'clock today."

He walks around the room and hands back our test papers. Mine is a D.

"Doyle, you still have a chance to get a C on your report card," he says. "Make sure you do the extra assignment after school."

I look at the board. I have to get on the Khan Academy, complete lesson sixteen, and pass the test.

AFTER SCHOOL. I only have two hours.
I run to the library, find a
computer, and get on the Khan
Academy.

Perry walks in on his crutches
and sits next to me. He's been
helping me in math after school for
the last two weeks.

"Let me know if you need help,"
he says.

"Thanks," I say. "But I have to
do this on my own. It's a special
assignment. I have to finish the
work and pass the test to get a C on
my report card."

I begin working. The lesson is
hard. I try to work quickly. But it
takes time.

I look at the clock. There's only
one hour left.

I keep working.

Something happens.

The lights go off.

The computers shut down.

I wait for the power to come back on.

Nothing.

Perry opens his backpack and pulls out his laptop.

"Doyle, take this and run home," he says. "Get the lesson done and take the test. I know you can do it."

I sprint out the door and run as fast as I can.

HOME. I open the door, rush to the kitchen table, and turn on Perry's laptop.

The clock says 4:18. I have forty-two minutes.

I begin working. It's hard.

I finish the lesson. But I only have fourteen minutes left.

There are ten test questions. I have to get eight of them right.

The first seven are easy. I answer all of them correctly.

But I miss question eight. I also miss question nine.

It's almost five o'clock. I begin question ten. I have to get it right.

I choose my answer and click.

It's over.

I passed!

Now I can practice with the track team.

19 GREAT DAY

SATURDAY MORNING. I wish I could keep sleeping. But the sun shines in my eyes.

There's a knock on my door.

"Doyle, good news," Mr. Jensen says. "We just got word. You get to see your mom today."

I jump out of bed and get dressed.

I can't wait to see her.

But I'm also worried.

What will she look like?

What will she say?

What if I fall apart?

Mario and Inez are already at the table when I get to the kitchen.

"I'm glad for you, bro," Mario says. "I know what it's like."

"Me too," says Inez. "I'm glad you get to see your mom today."

The tears start coming.

I look away.

Mrs. Jensen puts her arm around me.

MID-MORNING. I sit in the front seat next to Mr. Jensen. He gets off the freeway and turns right.

The sign on the street says Vernon County Jail.

My heart pounds.

"I know you're nervous," Mr. Jensen says. "But it's going to be okay."

We get to the visitors' center
and stand in line.

An officer with rubber gloves
searches me.

He does the same for Mr. Jensen.

I feel like a prisoner.

ONE HOUR LATER. A voice comes over
the loudspeaker and calls us to door
number three.

A guard takes us into a special
room. It has glass booths with
telephones where prisoners and
visitors can talk to each other.

We go to our booth.

Mom comes in and sits across the
glass from us. She's smiling and
looks better now.

We pick up our phones.

"Doyle," she says. "I'm so glad
to see you. I've been so worried."

"I'm fine," I say. "But I've been
worried about you."

"I don't like it here," she says.
"But I can make it. When I get out,
we'll be back together again. That's
what keeps me going."

Suddenly, I feel better.

We talk about everything. I tell
her about the Jensens, about school,
and about Perry helping me.

Thirty minutes pass.

Mr. Jensen and I have to leave
now.

But I feel better.

Things are going to be okay.

BACKYARD. Mr. Jensen cooks
hamburgers on the barbecue. Mario
and I stand next to him.

"Mr. Jensen," I say. "Do you know
that burgers are my favorite food?"

"I knew you had good taste," he says. "They're my favorite, too."

He turns to face me. "Don't forget," he says. "My first name is James. Whenever you're ready, you don't have to call me Mr. Jensen."

I don't know if I can do it. But I'll try.

AFTER DINNER. Mario and I shoot hoops on the driveway.

He shows me how to put spin on the ball.

I make a ten-footer.

He tosses me the rebound.

I make another shot.

Things are better now.

It's been a great day.

20 JUST LIKE PERRY

WEDNESDAY MORNING. Edison High School. Mario and I walk through the front gate. It's the second day of the spring semester.

Two years have passed since I came to live with the Jensens.

I'm a senior now. I graduate in June.

Mom is still in prison. But she'll be out next year.

"Doyle, how was track yesterday?" Mario asks.

"Pretty good. I think I'll be

running the 200 and 400 meters this year."

"Have you heard anything from Munson State?" he asks.

"Not yet. But the coach there says I have a good chance for a scholarship."

It would be nice to go to Munson.

But Jasper Community College would also be fine.

They have a good track team. They also have a program for future teachers.

ALGEBRA TWO. Mr. Braden comes to the front of the classroom and writes a problem on the board.

He pulls a card out of his name jar. "Teresa, could you come up and solve it?"

She walks to the front and tries.

But she can't do it.

Mr. Braden pulls another card out of his name jar. "Doyle, could you come up?"

I walk to the front, complete the problem, and explain how I did it.

"Good job," Mr. Braden says. "That was very clear."

STUDY HALL. I enter the room and take my seat. I'm a peer tutor now.

The person I'm assigned to is a new kid, Allen.

He shows me his latest math test. It's a NoPass.

"Don't worry," I say. "Math used to be my worst subject. But I'm good at it now. Open up your book. I'll watch as you work."

He reads the problem and writes

down a bunch of numbers. But he has no idea what he's doing.

"That's okay," I say. "Things are going to get better for you."

Allen looks down and says nothing.

It feels like he's given up on himself.

But I'm not going to let that stop me.

I'm going to keep trying with Allen, just like Perry kept trying with me.

ACKNOWLEDGMENTS

I would like to express my sincere appreciation to everyone who gave me feedback while I was writing this book.

COFFEE HOUSE WRITERS GROUP: Gourav Acharya, Noemi Arellano-Summer, Daniel Burns, Renee Carter, Nicholas Chiazza, Dan Cragan, Nick Cruz, Jessica Evans, John Goshorn, Lynne Horn, Darian Lane, Jean Pliska, Steve Hovland, Peter Ingersoll, Yumiko Jubami, Eugene Mendelcorn, Patti Mobile, Carson Mogk, Jean Pliska, Katherine Ralson, Jared Reed, John Steiner, Stephen Van Fossen, Michael Vincent, Ron Wolff, and Min.

SOCIETY OF CHILDREN'S BOOK WRITERS AND ILLUSTRATORS: Jude Atwood, Betsy Barker, Tim Burke, Angela Cerrito, Jennifer Chiou, Carlene Griffith, Christine Henderson, Erin Lagerberg, Rommy Nelson, Molly O'Neill, Jennifer Parsons, Kelly Powers, Jodi Rizzotto, Shiva Sadeghi, Crystal Schreck, Desi St. Amat, Suzanne Sutton, Charlotte Van Ryswyk, Joyce Wyels.

Thank you, Pam Sheppard, for your advice on creating this series.

Thank you, Laura Perkins, for your feedback and careful editing.

Thank you, Betty Jean, for your patience, your wisdom, and for being my wife.

ABOUT THE AUTHOR

My dream of becoming a writer started at Whitworth College. I was lucky to have a teacher, Dr. Tammy Reid, who believed in me and encouraged me. After college, I began a career as an educator, teaching reading and English at a middle school in Los Angeles. I went to college at night to earn a doctorate in education. I then served as a high-school principal and district administrator. One of the most important things I have learned is that everyone can achieve success. Set your sights high, work hard, and never give up. Strive to be the best that you can be.

FINDING FORWARD BOOKS

At Finding Forward Books, we publish easy-to-read novels about real issues and teens overcoming challenges in their lives. Our goal is to help students improve their reading skills, increase their success in school, and develop positive attitudes.

The books are suitable for all students, including English Learners and those with learning disabilities. Lexile measures range from 390 to 560.

They have been praised in *Kirkus Reviews*, *Publishers Weekly BookLife Reviews*, *Foreword Clarion Reviews*, and *BlueInk Reviews*.

ADDITIONAL TITLES

TAKEN AWAY. A teen learns to cope after his dad is sent to prison.

NO PLACE TO HIDE. A discouraged teen improves his reading skills.

NEVER WANTED. A neglected teen is placed in a foster home.

ALL ALONE. A teen learns to deal with his mom's alcoholism.

KNOCKED DOWN. A football player learns the importance of honesty.

TORN. A student with everything learns to care about another student who has nothing.

OVERSPRAY. A teen experiences grief after his father dies.

BLUE WALL. A troubled teen battles back from depression.

LETTERZ. A teen struggling with dyslexia learns how to succeed in school.

CANS. A teen who dreams of attending college struggles against poverty.

Finding Forward Books
Short Novels for Teens About
Issues Faced by Teens
www.findingforwardbooks.com